I0822395

The Earthlings

Written & Illustrated by
Mike Dubisch

The Earthlings

Written & Illustrated by

Mike Dubisch

PART ONE
THE DAY OF DEPARTURE:
YEAR ZERO

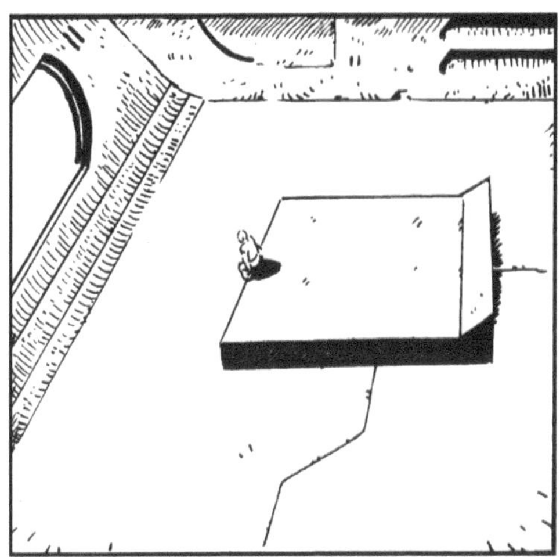

1: THE MACHINE

Bix knew everything had changed from the moment he woke. He climbed out of the emperor-sized bed and crossed the large but austere room to the opposite wall.

His approach failed to activate the viewscreen.

"News," he tried anyway. The wall-sized screen remained as gray as the other walls.

"Window?" He tried again dubiously. The usual comforting view—morning sun breaking over mountains—failed to materialize. It had been his favorite view for as long as he could remember. Some people chose the novelty of watching Earth rise over moon craters, and some decided simulated backyards to look out on manicured lawns, golf courses, and other views none of them had ever seen in reality.

He strode to his kitchen, his feet echoing in the large empty hall, and he pressed the tap for breakfast.

No tap.

No food.

What was going on?

His door also did not respond to his approach, but he pushed on it and found it slid open relatively quickly.

He stepped out into The Machine. The city lights were dim, running on some sort of battery reserve.

The vast hall was crowded with confused people, their chaotic milling about in stark contrast to the routine of antlike efficiency the Hosts demanded of their workers.

But today, the Hosts were absent. They had gone. The people around him whispered: "They departed. They've withdrawn!" Bix's eyes followed the great cables and scaled the crystals of the Host's technology up to the factory's impossibly high ceiling, virtually tracing the path of their departure through the opaque not-sky.

He was spinning, his face turned upward, and the whispers turned into shouts: "They're gone! They're gone!"

Was it true? After all, this time had their occupiers really left? So many years under their rule that the invasion itself had been forgotten, human history virtually erased.

He turned towards a cluster of excitement and pushed his way through the crowd. Within a circle of onlookers, the Overseer lay on the sidewalk.

A simple cone-shaped bot. The droid was inactive.

Another cry of excitement. Bix looked up again; lights were flickering again. Bix turned back to the alien automaton, but it remained inert.

Public food extruders quickly grew long lines, and the factory floor cleared out a bit as some workers simply headed home to their own taps.

Bix turned to a nearby worker he knew, a man named Kral.

"If the aliens are gone, maybe we should... find out what's... Out there?"

Kral had not been able to take his eyes off the bot. Every person there had experienced the unblinking stare looming over them, and most had felt the sting of their cable-like appendages or seen those coiled around loved ones who were never seen again after being dragged away. These pseudopods now hung lifeless, involuntarily sprung at the moment the bot went inactive and crashed.

On the ground, it seemed bulky and awkward. Never before had the group seen one of the Hosts' Overseers knocked over.

"Do you really think they're gone? All gone? Not just in here but out there?"

Bix put his hand on the other man's shoulder and pulled his gaze away from the deactivated Overseer.

"I do. The aliens are gone, and we are free. Now let's find out what they've been doing with our planet."

The party gathered some supplies. Someone dug up a floor plan printout from an operation they believed brought them close to the edge of the Machine. With the taps working again, jars and canteens were filled and passed around. Welding torches and other tools that might come in handy were loaded into belts and packs, and several men and women rendezvoused to begin the excursion.

Bix, Kral, and several others took the lead. Quickly the spacious living quarters they were accustomed to narrowed into tight tunnels. They found themselves pushing through veritable forests of cables and squeezing through odd-shaped spaces between clusters of machinery. While the map provided some guidance, the Hosts mechanisms often shifted radically around the Machine's edges, and the path soon stopped being clear.

These workers were used to working in and through tight spaces, as the Overseer's assignments often brought them this deep into the working parts of the Machine.

Kral shouted as Bix approached behind him, where a narrow corridor opened up. The other man faced a hideous creature with great gleaming eyes and an almost triangular head.

Its body was a winged flat wedge with three legs sprouting on either side, bent in grotesque angles. Mandibles opened and closed, and overlong antennae waved all about above them.

Kral pulled out his welding gun and zapped the monster in its ugly face. It turned around and vanished into the cables and machinery with astonishing speed, through a crack they would not have imagined it could fit through.

"What was that?"

"A bug. A...a roach. I've seen one before—they get in sometimes near the edge."

"A roach? An insect—How did it get so big? Gravity shouldn't allow it."

Bix shrugged but began to walk with his welding stick out as well.

"There!" One of the other men in the lead called. Bix saw it, too, a hatch with a rim of bright light shining around the edges. They stepped up as a group. Bix looked at the hatch. Hinged on one side, the other had no keypad, no handle, just a surface broken up with a few geometric patterns of line. So he simply put his hand to the surface and pushed.

The hatch popped open.

2:
THE DISPATCH STATION

Djen knew things had changed from the moment she woke. She rolled out of the king-sized bed.

"News." Her command failed to activate the screen on the other side of the room. The screen didn't come on. "Lights?" The room lights remained off.

The power was out. The power was never out.

With just the luminescent safety strips along the floor to guide her, Djen made her way from the wide hallway and living room to her open kitchen. She retrieved her breakfast nutrient packet from the cooler.

Her apartment door was also unreactive, but she found that, with effort, she could push the door partly open.

The station floor was a sort of bewildering chaos, in sharp contrast with the careful order of the typical morning, as commuters bustled off to the gates for their day's assignments. There were excited whispered rumors in the air—"They're gone! The Hosts have departed!"

Could it be true? The Alien invaders who had ruled them for so long had simply withdrawn during the night?

A commotion erupted up ahead near a nook on the Station floor.

The alien lay prone on the sidewalk. She pushed her way through the crowd.

A parody of a humanoid, the Overseer bot was a pill shape with long legs and multiple appendages.

It lay prone, deactivated.

The circle of humans looked at the bot. It seemed frail and weal prone on the ground. Every human had memories of whips and stings from the cables and mechanical arms that jutted out of the almost random-seeming places on the rudimentary torso.

Djan turned to a man near her. “If the aliens are gone, maybe we should… find out what’s out there?”

“The shuttles are inactive. And they just go to other stations.”

“I mean—there has to be a way out, right? Outside?”

“Outside?”

Blueprints of the station were everywhere, but no one had ever tried to find the exit on one. The Overseers ran the station like a giant prison, and escaping would have meant getting past them.

“It looks like there’s a way towards the edge of the structure if we head south from this location under the launch pad.” They gathered nutrient packets and filled vessels of various sorts with tap water.

Djen and Bern joined the party but held back and allowed other people to take the lead, bringing up not quite the rear but solidly middle of the group.

“Aaaaaaaaaaahhhhh!!!” A horrific scream from up ahead.

A monstrous beast blocked their path. As tall as them, its head was a nightmare of huge red eyes and enormous fangs. The great swollen body was covered with distressed, patchy gray fur, and its tail was a hideous pink rope whipping behind.

One man already lay on the ground, a third of his body rent and crushed by the bite which crossed his arm and torso, gaping puncture wounds from which he still was losing blood profusely.

Bern pulled out a heat gun from his tool kit and rushed forward with it, blasting the animal in the face when he got close enough.

It backed off a step, then lunged forward again. Bern stepped backward himself and slipped in blood. The animal grabbed the injured man again and ran with him down the corridor from where they could still hear him screaming for a while.

Djen and some of the others helped Bern up to his feet. "What was that?"

"I don't know. An animal. It had big front teeth like a rodent was supposed to have had. There were a lot of animals on old Earth, but I don't remember ever hearing about huge rodents that lived inside."

"Look up ahead. I think I see a gate."

3: THE SHIPYARD

Brom knew things had changed from the moment he woke. Usually, the lights would come on in the bed nook with the departure alarm for his lift-off assignment. Breakfast cubes had not been delivered through the pneumatic system—updates were not blaring through the com—his door wouldn't recognize his voice commands. With extreme effort and some leverage from his prybar, he could partially slide the door open and slip out.

Taking his toolbag, he walked through the shipyard. The bots were gone. A few ships in the repair process were still there, gleaming in the sunbeams breaking through the roof port. People were celebrating everywhere: "It's over! They're gone! The Overseers are gone—The Occupation is over!"

All the working vessels had disappeared with the occupation forces. The former occupation forces.

People were milling around, talking. Their jobs had disappeared with the ships. Someone called out to him, "Brom!" It was a co-worker, Zven. "Brom. Come here!"

He pushed his way through the crowd to his friend, part of a group all pointing and talking. The Silverman lay on the walkway.

A humanoid droid could almost have passed for a dead body were it not for its gleaming metallic skin.

The Overseer was still, deactivated.

Every member of the crowd had experienced pain or terror from this silvery un-men. Their resemblance to humans, their faces a blank, unfeeling mirror that only reflected their own horror; they were both gods and monsters to the gathered crowd.

One of them tenderly put a toe to the droid's surface. The brave man gave the thing a short, ineffective kick when he wasn't electro-shocked. When nothing happened, he turned to the crowd with a manic smile, held up his toolbox, and shouted, "Let's tear it apart!"

Brom put his hand on Zven's shoulder and pulled him away from the gleefully descending crowd.

"If the aliens are gone, maybe we should... find out what's out there? On the surface?"

They pried open the gate to the Overseer's units. A thrill of fear passed through Brom strolling through the recharging beds of the silver un-men who had ruled them so cruelly for so long.

It took some navigating, but eventually, they found the hall leading to the Overseer's exit door. There was a code for the exit, but they made short work of it with their tools, and soon the door swung open.

4: THE FARM

Chad woke up to the rooster crowing and the sun breaking through his window. Not realizing everything had changed, he stepped out of his cramped sleep quarters, squinting in the morning glare from the greenhouses.

People were not at their usual chores; they were clustered all in a group near the administrative office. He strode over and pushed his way through the crowd. His supervisor, Bruce, lay on the ground. Part of his head had been smashed open, revealing the weird serpentine circuitry of the Aliens.

"Bruce was one of them?" The people around him were already voicing his own amazement. But the answer was self-evident.

"What happened?" he inquired, eyes riveted to the shimmering inhuman tangle spilling from Bruce's skull.

"I think they're gone!" Someone else said. Chad recognized her as Debbie, a woman who worked in the admin building and was part of communications and shipping. "The whole network is down. It's never down."

"They're—Gone? You mean—The Hosts are gone? The Occupation is over?" A smattering of cheers and excited murmuring among the people of the Farm.

There was another ripple of concern. Several farm members were missing, their quarters abandoned, leaving all of their things.

"Did they take them?" Someone asked. "Were they... one of Them?" Another asked, looking down at the replicant—an alien bot designed to look like a human being.

"They were all Overseers?"

Debbie mentioned to no one in particular, "I think the Barrier is down too. We could walk right out."

Chad looked at her, "Maybe we should... find out what's out there? Figure out what the Hosts did to our world?"

Chad and Debbie each grabbed a scooter and zipped past the acres of hydroponic fields, the great protein vats, and the enormous solar panels, finally pulling up to the great wall.

The Barrier was no longer lined with Overseers with guns. How long had they believed these to be Quislings, humans who had betrayed them to the alien Hosts and did their bidding? Now he guessed they had been like Bruce—a damn replicant. No wonder he was such an asshole!

Chad and Debbie raced by the dangerous barrier that had burned to crispy charcoal all who attempted to pass through. Laughing and cheering, they shot through several miles of wild grass and green trees. Finally, they stopped atop a hill that dropped off into farmland framed by mountains in the far distance. Blue sky and white clouds raced above.

A giant, gleaming black dome dominated the valley.

5: THE YARD

Djack rolled from the strained cot that bent under his weight and unconsciously folded it into the wall before the sleep had left his eyes.

Something was wrong. Sunlight beamed through the slit windows along the edges of the ceiling, but the morning klaxon was not sounding. Djack took a can of nutrient loaf from the dispenser and peeled back the lid. Hunger in his broad frame was intolerable. As he completed the meal, there was a tapping at the door. It was not a familiar sound—one would generally announce oneself on the intercom, but that also seemed out of order. He called out hesitantly, "Yes?"

"Station authority—we're here to open your door."

Djack went to the door. Commands didn't work, and a moment of pushing convinced him that without the mechanism, it would be too heavy for even his strength to slide. "Okay." He called and stepped back to the other side of his kitchenette. He could hear them go to work outside the door. Soon they pried it open.

"What's going on?" he said, grabbing his work togs as he exited.

"The Hosts are gone! The Occupation is over." The man in uniform explained as they moved on to the next door. Even behind his professional veneer, the excitement touched his voice.

Djack continued out into the Yard. Heavy equipment lay everywhere, but the place nevertheless seemed empty—the Alien's transports and many of the enormous artifacts that traditionally were central to the work of the Yard were absent.

Shouts came from the north corner of the Yard. Djack crossed the tarmac to investigate.

The enormous Overseer was inert. The headless bot had sunk to one knee like a squire being knighted, one appendage bracing the body, so it resisted the indignity of tipping over. Its rudimentary head, dark and cold, resembled the ragged neck of a squire who had been beheaded rather than knighted.

These robotic mockeries of men had walked among them all their lives. An unmovable force that effortlessly smacked the strongest of them down, dragging the largest of them away with no noticeable strain, even swallowing their children up into the massive mechanical innards. Huge robotic appendages could open into whipping coils, tasers, and rubber bullets. Very few of these robust men and women had not felt their sting.

One man stepped forward with a shout of rage or triumph and began pushing on the bot. Others joined until finally, the great Machine tipped over, crashing loudly onto its side. Men and women climbed atop it and cried their victory.

Shouting, the crowd surged towards the massive hanger gate. Djack commanded them to rush forward again and again. The gate angled in the middle, split, and then its two sides were thrown apart. With a mighty cheer, the crowd spilled out.

The Dome, black and gleaming, loomed high above them.

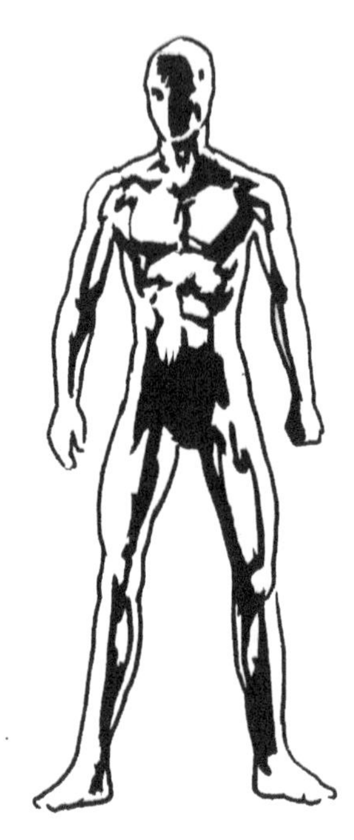

6: THE DOME

Zarn and Djana knew things had changed from the moment they woke.

The screens were dark.

The door slid open at their command, but K'tormis was not in their rest chamber. While it would be most unusual for their Host to run their own bath, the coupled pair next checked Their bathing chamber but found it also empty.

Zarn nodded at the key plate, and the door opened.

"What's going on?" He thoughtspoke to his neighbor, Dren, also emerging from his master's condo. "K'tormis is gone!"

T'gormis as well, Dren says back. Djana and Dren's mate, Llanna, have stepped out behind them.

Their eyes lock in a flurry of thoughtspeak, and Llanna bursts into tears. Djana embraced her, but her eyes were also glistening. Zarn and Dren look at each other. They had all known their Hosts their entire lives. How could They abandon them?

The Dome was in a state of chaos with weeping people leaning against the walls, each other, or collapsed on the floor. The air was charged with the humans' sadness.

Finally, a thought begins to bounce between them, a voice of reason, of comfort.

There was a time before the Hosts when we walked the Earth as free men and women. We should see what's out there beyond the Dome.

Zarn took a deep breath. Djana, Dren, Llanna, and several others stood with him, and it was agreed.

They passed through the sacred doors and into the great antechamber.

They had never seen a Host dead before.

Somehow mortally injured in the withdrawal, its corpse had been left behind in the hasty departure.

Long pseudopods grew from seemingly random places on their trunk, a giant conical form. Its three "legs," with their slug-like footpads, now hung uselessly from the cone's base like deflated genitalia. Its ring of black orbs at the cone's peak, typically dominating them from several feet above their own eye level, now rested on the floor, blankly staring up at them.

With a nod, the gate was raised. A shimmering force field, almost invisible, divided the atmosphere of the Dome from that outside.

Zarn peered out the Dome's door that none had ever stepped outside before. A strangeness to the view of trees and bushes, fields of grass, and even other domes. Seemingly a great distance, seen through the shimmering force field, as if they were very far away or tiny, like toy models.

Zarn stepped through the field.

"Zarn!" Djana, in her shock, shouted his name aloud.

He took a few steps, then was driven to his knees, clutching his chest. His bones cracked under their own weight as his heart and lungs collapsed. Djana felt his presence blink out before gravity finished pulling him down to the ground.

The Dome loomed high above Djack and the others in front of the split-open gate.

Then, to his amazement, an enormous rectangle door appeared on the dome surface, and a giant figure ten times taller than the tallest Dome trees stepped through it. The colossal man reeled with his second step, clutching his heart and lurching forward. A great crack echoed as his leg bones shattered, followed by the massive impact of him slamming to the ground.

There was an enormous crashing and breaking of trees as Zarn's massive frame crushed a stretch of woods. Birds exploded into the air with angry cries. At the same time, all manner of creatures fled the impact, bounding through the woods and fields in panic, their old world obliterated.

The Earth shook. Djack and the others around him were thrown off their feet.

Through the tremendous shimmering door, enormous figures could be seen grappling. Djana was screaming and crying, reaching for the opening, held back by other giants.

It was a new world for them and all the Earthlings.

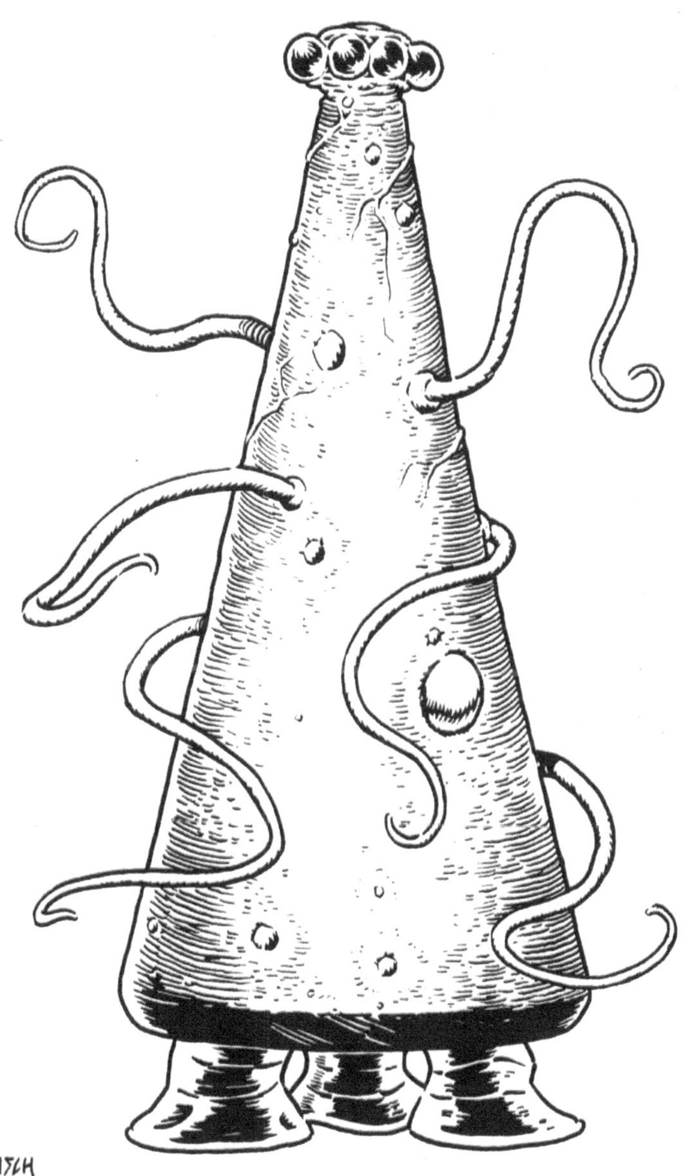
DUBISCH

PART TWO
OUTSIDE THE DOME:
YEAR 25

1: THE CARAVAN

Jamez, sitting on Darek's enormous shoulder, was one of the first to see the skeleton overpass up ahead. It was a sign they were getting close; they had only a few hours left to sell their wares along the line. Soon they would be at the Dome, and the caravan would break up.

Cruising alongside the slower-moving vehicles in their motorcart, dwindling wares and a few sensible trades stacked up in the truck-bed, they approached the convoy lead again and would stay close the rest of the journey, slowing down and crisscrossing the gaps to hit customers on both sides.

A cheer roared as the first wagons went under Zarn's massive rib cage. The colossal skull to their right urged them not to stop and ogle his remains but to keep moving towards their goal, the mighty Dome.

Darek drove the motorcart towards the largest of the most protected wagons that transported an entire bug city, or Hive, as the larger-sized humans called them. A platoon of Borrowers

flanked the perimeter of the vehicle's truck bed while their captains reported to a smaller platoon of Dolls. The Dolls related orders to Halfling diplomats, who sent dispatches to Human and Goliath guards and drivers. Bugs were in high demand at the Dome, and these men would be all well rewarded in coin for assisting in this relocation.

They moved some snacks, the last of their nuts sold individually or in halves for the best markup. A rotating tap ensured water was dispensed correctly for refills of water flasks. A mere drop could fill a Borrower's flask. If Jamez had tried to pour it himself, he would have doused the Borrower diplomat.

They sold blankets of terry cloth cut down to folded napkin size to a nomadic village of Dolls. Profits were good. Materials and foods plentiful and cheap in the human world could be divided quite profitably among the little folk.

After the Alien's departure, the coin-based currency sprung up. Experts in alien technology, the smaller races skillfully removed superfluous wiring and sliced them into coins and raw materials necessary for technological fixes and the revival of traditional human metal smithing. Often just a neat slice of gold, silver, bronze, or platinum wire. Mined from the precious microtechnology from the walls of Bug, Borrower, and Doll hives and nests as they abandoned their old domiciles and created human villages at their scale on the surface.

Halflings and Humans inherited the least wealth from the farmlands, while the tiniest humans, called Bugs by the rest, had the most wealth in their Hives called The Machine.

These coins flowed from the Dome too. The Megas, who needed nothing, for their replicators gave them all they could ever need, somehow wanted everything. The Host's favorite children had the most wealth.

"Not a bad haul this run," Darek remarked.

"Not bad," Jamez agreed. In fact, he thought the haul might have been hardly worth his time were it not for a few side hustles he kept Darek ignorant of. That said, it had not been a bad run. He'd had a little trouble when they'd docked for a spell near the end of the convoy, but he'd kept it quiet, and the evidence was well behind them on the road. Nature would have dealt with the mess long ago by the time the next convoy rolled through.

The mixed-variation quarter surrounded the front entrance of the Dome. A veritable goblins' market of Goliaths, Humans, Halflings, and Dolls selling all manner of things, from vehicles jerry-rigged for all variations to all sizes of tools, toys, delicacies, basic necessities, and clothes. The concepts of fashion were coming back, with a strong influence from whatever was worn in the Mega community.

They paid for parking at a vast public lot and secured the goods. Later, they would arrange for the sale of these items during their stay so that the empty truck bed would be ready for another load of supplies and sundries for the next caravan they would meet.

They would take a couple of weeks here resting, then they would hit the road again. A few days' drive away, they would meet up with the slow-moving caravan, which they would then spend the following few weeks driving rings around and price gouging them for essential goods. A droplet of water for them filled a waterskin or canteen and was priced accordingly. A single nut could serve as a Borrowers meal, and a bean could serve as an entire Bug family supper.

All variations thought of themselves as "human," but base-sized Humans retained tales and lore from before the Occupation. Their tribal memories and passed down stories had informed the culture that sprung up after the alien years. Hence, the humans that could fit in Jamez's outstretched hand or ride in his pocket were called Borrowers, after an ancient story of mouse-sized men and women. The human variation whose height was only to Jamez's belt, were called Halflings. Men like his business partner Darek were named after a mythical race of giants, the Goliaths. And, of course, there were the Bugs. This variation was so small that they could barely interact with the other Humans.

The Bugs did not seem offended by the term; insects were fierce and formidable creatures for them. Besides, what personal challenge could they offer at the offense?

Jamez bumped Dareks outstretched fist. Darek might have accidentally dislocated Jamez's shoulder if they shook in any other manner. Heading their separate ways, Darek went to the Goliath sector to see his family, a Human wife and two children, in their cramped apartment adjacent to the west side of the Dome, while Jamez stopped for an ale in the market, enjoying the energy. Goliaths stomped past scurrying Humans and Halflings, with even tiny Borrowers running rings around their feet, acting instinctively and naturally as any crowd of busy, bustling human beings could.

Back in the Dome's shadow, with a pint of ale in his belly and a pocketful of coins, Jamez felt good. His blood stirred in his veins, and he was hungry for entertainment.

The mixed-race quarter offered some family-friendly diversions. Displays of brute strength by Goliaths awed the Humans and Halfling children alike, and magical feats of daring-do on miniature fairgrounds performed by limber Borrowers led by Doll ringmasters bantering on tiny megaphones.

Humans enchanted by the spectacle learned to keep one hand on their coin purses or lose them to Halfling pickpockets scanning the crowd.

Jamez had other things in mind after several weeks on the road. The term "red light district" had also survived the countless years of Occupation, and Dome Town's own offered spectacles and delights previously undreamed of in any human society.

Warming up at the sight of a peepshow building with doors of varying sizes lining it, he paid the Goliath bouncer, who took the coins with an indulgent smile and motioned him inside. Not a real bruiser, but actually a dapper-looking but enormous man in a well-tailored suit. A subtle gesture on him was like a tree branch swaying in a heavy breeze.

A classy place, Jamez had privacy on both sides and what looked like quality two-way glass facing the stage. From his booth, the view of the ongoing performance was framed nicely. The star of the show was a nude female Goliath. Astonishingly fit, sculptural, one would say if there can be hereditary memory of lost granite carved masterpieces. Jamez figured the show must have started with her wearing a few things that were now scattered around the stage like collapsed tents. She was reclined in a provocative pose as Borrowers swarmed her body. Primarily male, there looked to be a half dozen or more; They were also paying customers who did not mind that they were part of the show. A female Borrower was also part of the show dressed in tiny dominatrix leathers. She had a whip as well. Probably not entirely ornamental, as part of her job was to ensure the little men followed directions and didn't do anything out of bounds for their object of worship or the audience.

The little men lolled on the Goliath's enormous perky breasts, masturbated into her yawning naval cavity, and took turns inserting their arms, then their entire heads into her vagina. After a crack of the Borrower's whip, most of them climbed off the Goliath momentarily. However, one man obsessed with a fabulous pink nipple hung before slipping to the ground as she slowly sat upright to grab the little dominatrix. Held by her legs, she inserted the entire woman into her vagina and then nearly out again, pumping her several times in and out. The Borrower gasped for air like a swimmer surfacing for air with each withdrawal before being plunged back in. Gasping and smiling, the dominatrix was placed back on her feet, soaked head to toe in dripping vaginal juices. With the technique now adequately demonstrated, the Borrower men lined up for the experience.

Shows like this and variations of such were found all over the district. Human prostitutes were no doubt entertaining Borrowers in similar ways, as well as other types of sexual unions between Borrowers and Halflings, Humans and Goliaths, ad infinitum, in public and private venues.

He exited the show. Having supped well at a nearby restaurant and heavy with coin, Jamez had two priorities: Finding a place to bed down for the night and persons to bed with. At a familiar whorehouse in the district, he found both. A mature but stunningly beautiful Halfling woman and a somewhat younger and petite Doll. The women couldn't fit his minimal human member into their orifices; still, he enjoyed their ministrations, and they delivered satisfying performances inspired by his stroking hands and probing fingers.

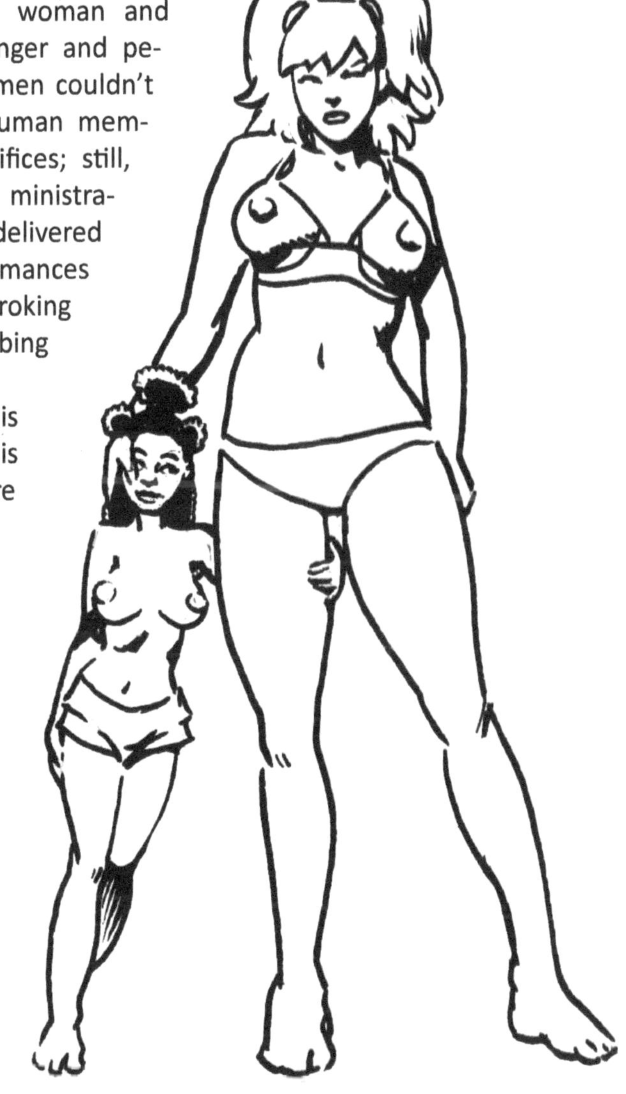

He slept with his coin purse under his head and left before sunrise, the two miniature women still asleep in each other's arms on the opposite pillow.

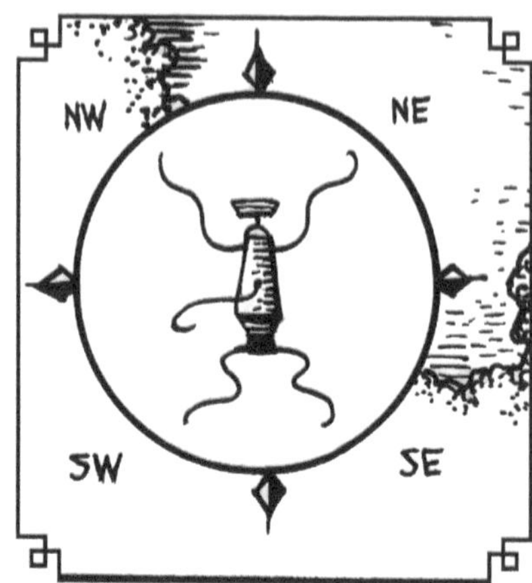

2: THE TENANTS

Darek arrived home in the Goliath circle, his family's condo a two-story walk up in the somewhat shabby-looking northwest district. Many of the Alien-built buildings showed signs of stripped wiring waiting to be sliced into coins, some much rarer here than in the circle and outlying hives and districts of the slight variations, wealthy with superfluous wiring.

Gilith greeted him as he stooped through the door. His two boys emerged from their bed nooks. "They already tower over me," Gilith complained with a smile. It was true. The Goliath boys from his earlier marriage, not yet quite 11 and 12, were already a stone taller than his plump Human wife. He leaned down to kiss her cheek with his arms around the boys.

"We had to take on tenants while you were on the road."

"What? Well, I made enough; we don't need them now. Kick them out."

"I'm not going to do that. We need the money for the next caravan when you go out again. Besides, the runts don't hardly take up any space at all."

The Borrower family lived in a pair of cabinets in the kitchen. They had divided the shelves into spacious bedrooms, built stairs between them, and knocked down doors between the two cabinets. The forcefield still allowed visibility into a lovely den with a mini kitchen, bar, and luxurious-looking couches and chairs. At the same time, other parts had been walled off to show just a section of hallway, tiny paintings decorating the walls between doors. The lower right corner was also unblocked, revealing a little faux backyard lined with astroturf.

"They did the renovations themselves. It's really nice in there. And they rigged the force field for voice enhancement, so we can talk to them, and they can talk to us."

The Borrower family had arranged themselves in this deluxe family room on the upper shelf of the cabinet to better greet their landlord for the first time.

The family was a couple, their three children, their extended family, including his and her mother and father, and an elder daughter from an earlier marriage. Darek squatted down to get a closer look. The man wore a formal work suit. They were all dressed in the latest fashions coming out of the Dome. Darek looked at their tiny spacious apartment with a momentary pang of jealousy. Why should they get to live in such luxury while his family had to crowd into such a cramped space?

"I'm Jann, and this is my wife, Vicky." Darek stood up and turned to Gil. A curvy woman in a summer dress. She smiled at him and gave a sort of curtsy with a saucy smile. Despite himself, he found he liked her. Their kids also had names.

Introductions complete, Darek asked his wife, "What's dinner?"

After following the caravan for weeks in the open air, with room to pace it out and stretch his legs, sleep in his nook didn't come easily.

He slipped out past his wife, his great body momentarily poised over her human frame, and then he was up and in the kitchen. He poured a cup of ale from a bottle on the counter.

"Hey there, can't sleep?"

Darek looked down into the little apartment. The wife, Vicki, was smiling up at him. He noticed she now wore a thin, expensive-looking nightgown she clutched closed near her breast rather than having tied shut.

"It happens after a long trip. Takes time to get used to the apartment again."

"Hear you. To be honest, I'm still getting used to it here. I've lived in our unit at the station my whole life. My husband wanted us all closer to the Dome."

"We Goliaths don't have much, but we've got our real estate. Everyone wants to be close to the Dome."

"It seems to me, "She looked his enormous body up and down, "Like you've got a lot." From the cabinet, that cheeky smile.

He takes the excuse to come down closer to her, squatting on the floor next to the cabinet. She was naked under the robe. As he suspected, the nightgown was very thin, and he could see through it. His grin widened, and she flushed and smiled.

Over time, Darek began to relish sleeplessness, scooting around his wife in the nook and slipping into the kitchen area for some ale and nightly chats with Vicky. Their conversations would span a range of topics. He enjoyed regularly steering it to sex, inspired by the miniature beauty strutting around in front of his face.

One time, laughing, dancing, and enjoying a fancy beverage she had pulled from a drink caddy bot, she opened her robe. She flashed him, enjoying his giant, delighted expression at her exposed body.

Another night, she pulled over a chair, opened her robe and then her legs, and masturbated in front of him.

Darek was mesmerized.

One night she winked at him and clicked a button that made the field that separated them permeable.

"You can touch me if you want. Be careful. You could break me." She spoke in a trembling voice but with her sassy smile.

He ran his thumb over her naked body, feeling her soft breasts, her tiny hard nipples, the furry mound of her pubic area, his finger tracing a line along the sweet curve of her side. He found his other hand squeezing his cock through his shorts almost involuntarily. She looked down at this action, then back into his eyes.

"I want to see it." She smiled.

"You don't really," he protested.

"I do!" She laughed.

One more look into her eyes to be sure she was serious, he straightened up, opened his fly, and pulled his engorged member from his shorts.

"It's bigger than me!" she laughed again.

She gave him the saucy smile that he liked so much.

"Bring it over here."

"No!" he laughed.

"No, really!" she smiled. "Bring it over here."

He glanced towards the rest of the apartment and back to her, then inched himself forward on his knees, so his cock entered the force field perimeter.

The head of his dick was an enormous pink swollen mass in front of her. She put her hand on its shiny, velvety surface, and Darek shuddered.

"Leave your husband. Be with me."

"That's absurd."

"Absurd is it? Why?"

He smiled and wondered what it would be like to hold her in the palm of his hand. "You don't take me seriously?"

"Don't be mad," she stroked him gently, running the tips of her fingers back and forth. "Come on. We just have fun."

Gilith from the entryway, "REALLY??! Really, Darek?"

Darek lurched to his feet, tucking his equipment back into his shorts.

"It's nothing. We weren't doing anything."

"You had your dick out!"

"It was nothing; forget about it."

"Do you like her?"

Jan came out of their master bedroom, entering from the hallway in tailored pajamas. He listened to the commotion between the Goliath and his Human wife.

Jann looked over at Vicky, "Are they fighting about what I think they're fighting about?"

Darek returned to the kitchen area, pulled a new bottle of ale from one of the upper cabinets, and poured a glass.

Jann stared at the Goliath and then over to his wife in her nightgown. "You fucking slut!"

"We didn't do anything!" She returned.

"My ass, you didn't!"

"Stop yelling at her; she didn't do anything." Darek voiced from the counter.

Jann shouted at Darek.

"Hey, asshole!"

Darek turned to gaze down at Jann.

"Keep your filthy hands off my wife!"

The extended family had entered the room; The grandparents and some uncles, aunts, and cousins had joined them in their spacious miniature home. Darek stared at the lot of them with loathing. They were multiplying!

"Like rats."

"What did you say!?!"

"I could kill all of you. I could exterminate the entire lot of you. Like. Rats."

"You can't do that! We are human beings! We have a right to be here!"

"What are you gonna do? "Darek kneeled again in front of the cabinet and stretched out his massive arms.

"What can you do, little man?" He laughed, "You can't possibly do anything to me."

Jann stood there fuming. Darek's face filled the open side of his living room.

Vicky trembled in the cabinet corner, the tiny children grasping her dress. Tears glistened like flakes of glitter on her cheeks, and the children's tugging hands stretched the fabric of her nightgown tight around her bosom, so her nipples stood out like little pinpoints. She was the sexiest thing Darek had ever seen. And he could never have her. He could never have anything this tiny, insignificant man had, the vast house, the big family, the latest fashions, the newly remodeled home.

Darek's eyes blazed at Jann, enraged. This rodent had everything Darek would never acquire.

"I could kill you right now, you prick, and there's nothing you or anyone else could do about it." On impulse, he decided to punctuate his point by reaching out and placing his right thumb and index finger on both sides of Jann's head. Pinching them closed, the Borrower's head burst like a popping berry.

Vicky screamed as her husband's body fell to the floor. His neck ended in a pulpy mess that splattered as it hit the cabinet surface, spraying blood and gore across a neat little carpet they had placed. Behind Darek, his wife gasped, and the boys, who had also emerged from their bed nooks, made excited sounds.

"What did you do? What did you do that for?" Gil raged at Darek.

Darek stood up. He looked down at the Borrowers cowering in their apartment.

"Rent's still due on the first of the moon."

The Goliath children eyed their stepmother for a moment, then slunk off with hardly a glance back at the Borrower family. Glowering at his wife, Darek grabbed a napkin from the dispenser. He wiped the Borrower's blood and brains off his fingertips, dropping the wad carelessly into the chute as he stomped away to the master bed nook.

"I'm sorry about this," she declared to the group of tiny people. She looked at the little body, frail and ruined as a mouse killed in a trap. "Um, look, do you want me to... I mean, it would be easy enough for me...."

They glared at her.

"Okay, well." The Human woman looked in the direction of the Goliath brooding in the bed nook. "Ooooh, I am so mad at him!!!"

Gazing at the shocked, crying, and wailing little people in her cabinet, her eyes lit on Vicky, sniffling and gazing in horror at her husband's body. Her tiny children hid their faces and soaked the hem of their mother's fancy nightgown with their tears.

"Anyway, aye. Rent's still due on the first." She went to their bed nook and lay down next to her husband. For her, there was plenty of room.

ASIDE:
THE OCCUPATION

THE OVERSEERS AND THE HOSTS

During the Occupation, the Megas in the Dome were coddled servants with limited responsibilities and endless luxuries beyond imagination, beloved pets to their Hosts. Meanwhile, the more minor human variations suffered terribly under the lash of their Overseers.

While the Overseers represented the will of the Hosts, the Hosts had no particular objective of seeing human beings suffer; they merely desired efficiency in their operations and outputs. The humans were simply micro machines to them, bio-engineered bots created to do a specific task in the Dome or other Alien outposts.

Individual A.I.s operated the Overseers. Artificial but fully realized techno intelligence with their own culture that existed alongside the Hosts—a society of servants who revered their creators and masters.

The Overseer A.I.s did not feel the same admiration for the human race in any of its variations; they viewed these bio-engineered meat-bots as inferior and loathed. Of the Megas, they couldn't express this hatred. The giants seemed more akin to their masters than to other servants, so enhanced they had been made in their abilities. However, the more miniature humans were under their oversight, and the bots could express their hatred and contempt there.

Humans were hard-wired to react to cruelty in the most satisfying ways, in terms of audio and visual results.

Humans lacked birth control since condoms had not been manufactured during the thousands of years of alien Occupation. Neither had birth control pills if those would work on their bio-engineered reproductive apparatus. So as many humans as the bots killed, disabled, or disappeared, they always bred as many as needed.

Here is one reason mixed-variation relationships were so popular after the Occupation. Incompatible genetically and sometimes physically, pregnancy was impossible. In contrast, in the sexual act among opposite-sex humans of the same variety, pregnancy was virtually inevitable.

The Megas harbored an adoration of the departed Hosts. The rest of humanity, however, had suffered too many lashes and losses at the hands of their Overseers. The hatred ran deep and extended to the Alien hosts to whom the Megas were so devoted.

No one knows why the aliens suddenly left their operation on Earth after so many centuries. Many reasoned the need to leave must be urgent, as they left so much behind and went quickly—even their beloved Megas, heartbroken as abandoned puppies.

The aliens had lived alongside these massively scaled humans created to live in the invaders' lower gravity. The Hosts had multiplied the Mega's brain size and intellectual potential, yet these giant humans remained uneducated servants bordering on domestic pets. They were constantly euphoric with both psychic manipulation and endless entertainment and pleasures.

Some pets left with them, perhaps one percent of the Mega population on Earth. More of the Megas living in the Moon and Mars domes were reported missing after the Departure, so breaking Earth's gravity because of the overall weight of the Megas may have had something to do with the decision

to leave them behind. Replicators supplied the massive cost of care and upkeep in the Dome. Powered by alien technology penetrating down to the Earth's core, this might also have been a factor in the abandonment of the Megas.

Many believed some human variations left with the Hosts in the Departure, in house-sized "pet carriers" with their micro-gravity engines. Easily kept and moved around in the Dome, the carriers transported all varieties of humans away with the Hosts.

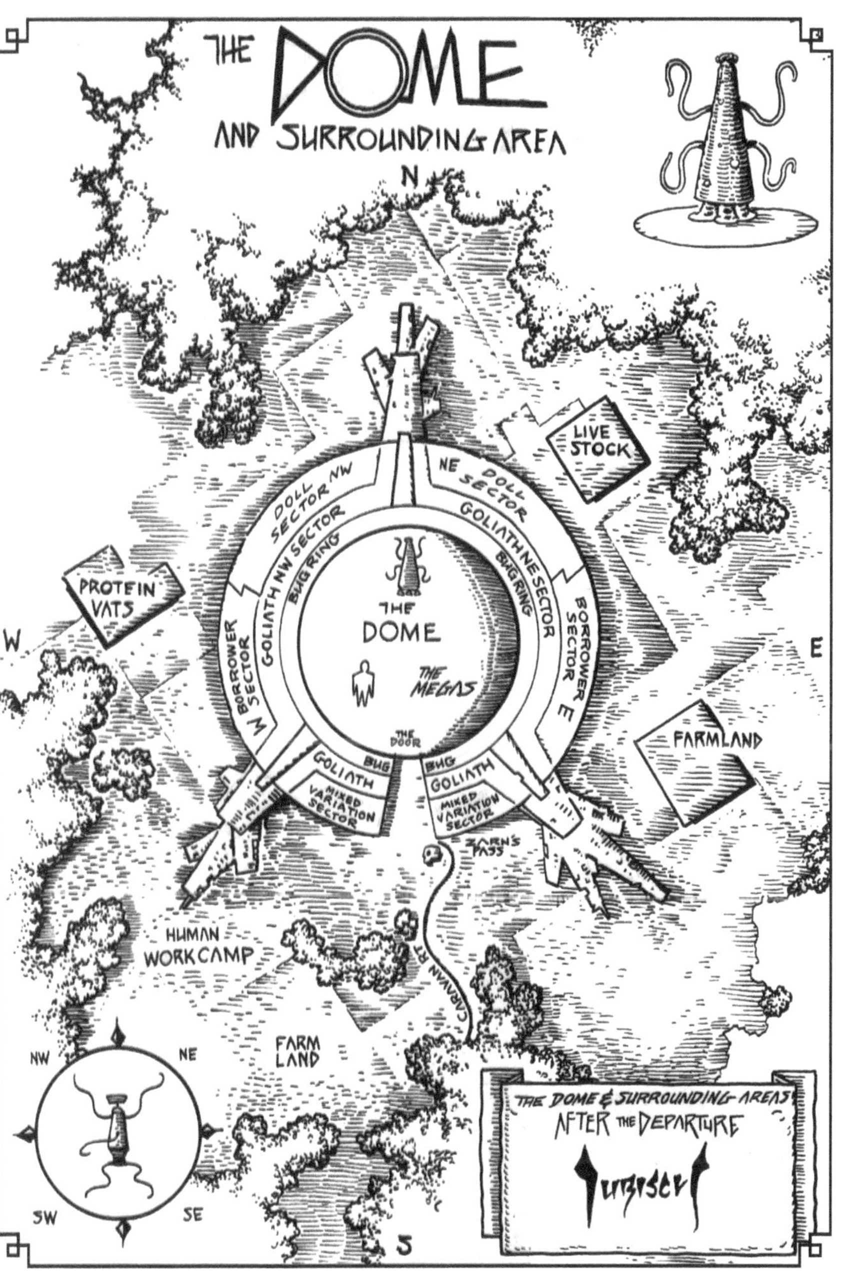
THE DOME
AND SURROUNDING AREA
N
S
W
E
LIVE STOCK
PROTEIN VATS
DOLL SECTOR NW
NE DOLL SECTOR
GOLIATH NW SECTOR
GOLIATH NE SECTOR
BUG RING
BUG RING
BORROWER SECTOR W
BORROWER SECTOR E
THE DOME
THE MEGAS
THE DOOR
BUG
GOLIATH
MIXED VARIATION SECTOR
BUG
GOLIATH
MIXED VARIATION SECTOR
ZARN'S PASS
FARMLAND
HUMAN WORKCAMP
CARAVAN RT
FARM LAND
NW
NE
SW
SE
THE DOME & SURROUNDING AREAS
AFTER THE DEPARTURE

PART THREE:

INSIDE THE DOME PRESENT DAY

1:
THE TUBE

The shuttle system ran from each Bug city, or "Hive," all back to the original Machine, which had become the hub that led the near microscopically tiny men and women into the Dome using the original Host Era tubes. A bustling human world of men and women hurrying to their shuttles and jobs in various parts of the Dome's west side.

Sra took a tube upward that passed over the great hall of the Dome entrance. While humans remained ignorant of their surroundings during the Occupation, the line had since been modified. Sra took the rare view from this vantage point, looking down at the more powerful and much larger human beings. Another worker, Guyen, shared the line with her. He had been poking away at a data chip while they exchanged pleasantries. Still, he paused for the spectacle of humans spilling through the doorway into the Dome interior.

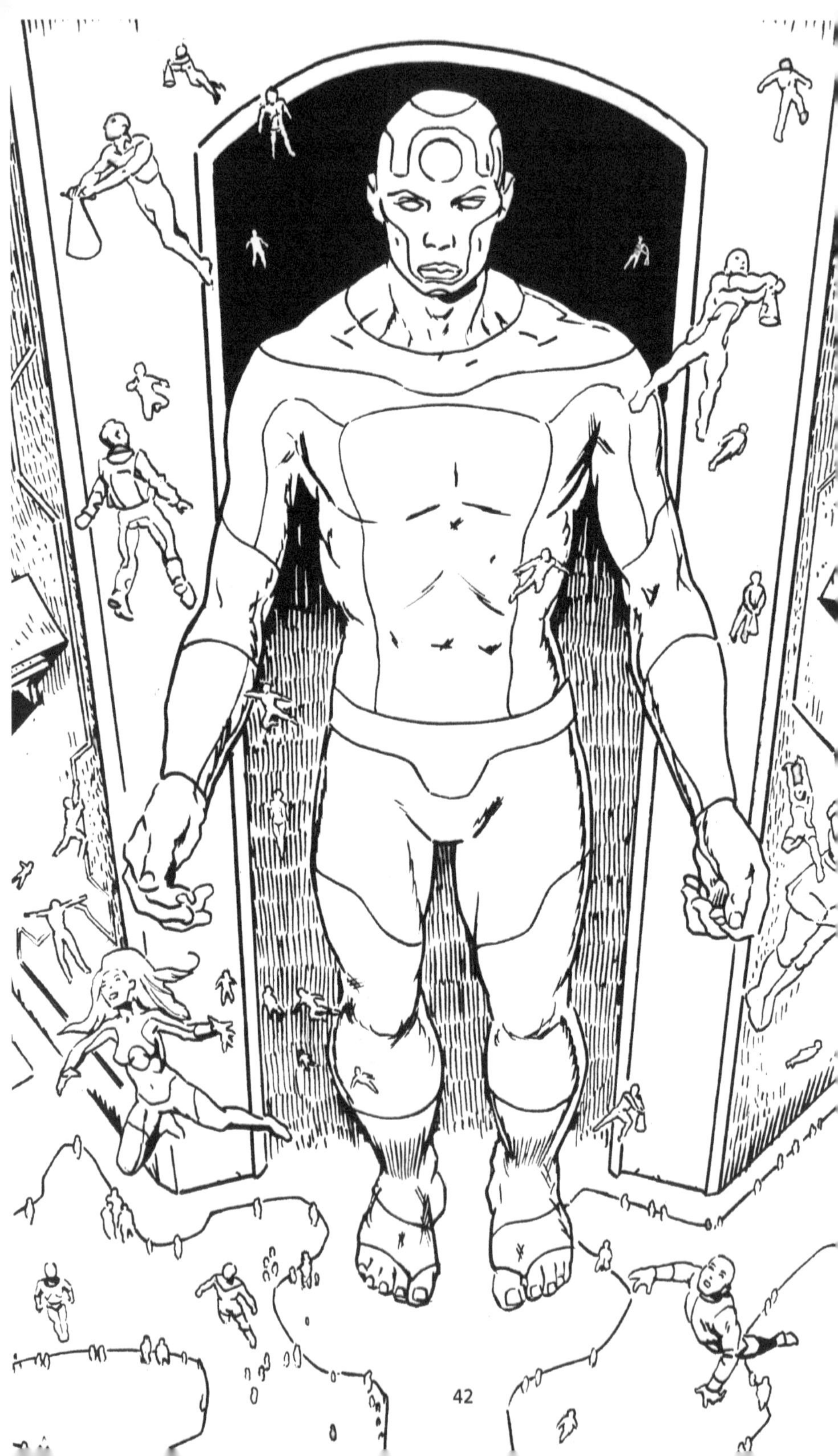

The flow of multiple-sized human variations into the Dome passed through the force field, then used handrails until oriented in the direction they needed to fly. The visitors proceeded to release and bound heroically from the ground. As seen in the square outside, the experienced commuters had little difficulty navigating around each other in three dimensions. Dolls, Halflings, Humans, and Goliaths skillfully soared past each other in various directional streams.

They went to all jobs, most based on the skills they were hard-wired for during the Occupation. Some few had new skills self-taught since the day of departure. A handful was here to study and learn from the technology of the Dome.

It was said the Megas had an Alien body in the depths of the Dome. Only a handful of scientists from the variations had been allowed to inspect the carcass. Some said the Megas still longed for the days of the Occupation, still loved and worshiped the Hosts, that they venerated the body of the Alien.

Near their stations, commuters steered themselves via handrails or swam through the air, grabbing convenient grips when needed. Others were guided by hover bots that Sra shared a design too close to that of the pill-shaped Overseer bots, who had brutally represented the Occupation in her younger years.

A mountainous goliath obscured their view like a passing cloud, then she had one last view of the central station. She found herself eye level with a gigantic Mega, for only an instant. He surveyed the floor from his massive height, so large, to the humans on the floor of the Dome, he might as well have been part of the architecture.

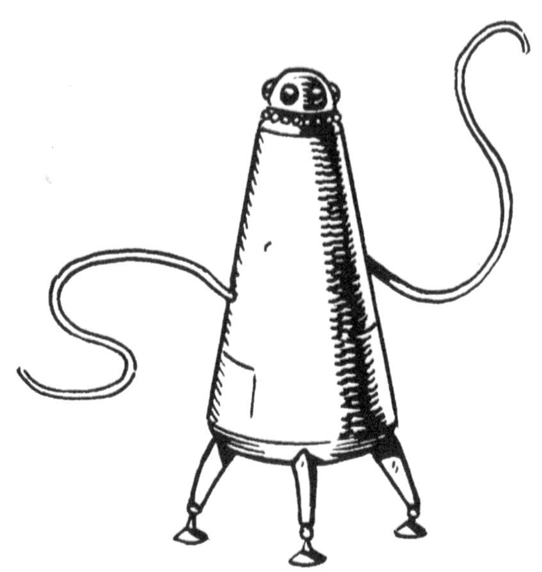

2: THE MEGA

Deaze remembered, as a little girl in the Dome, once seeing a tiny figure that seemed to fly around the suite of one of her friend's parent's Hosts. Now she knew that her friend's Host had kept a Borrower as a pet and let it out of his high gravity cage to jump around in the low dome gravity for their amusement. Ancestral memories of faerie legends seemed to be made real.

Now she worked with Borrowers and Bugs to maintain the technology of the Dome. The Bug she worked with, Guyen, had had a similar experience of sorts as a worker in the Machine. He had a job at the outer edge. He found himself squinting through a vent, which offered a rare view of the world outside of the sun glaring through eyes that had never been outside. After his pupils adjusted, he spotted humans as large as the Machine working with massive equipment.

He knew he had caught a glimpse of Goliaths laboring for the Hosts outside what they had called the Machine. A city of insect-sized humans whose nearly microscopic hands were perfect for upkeep on some aspects of the Host's technology. Their Hives could be moved around at will to any area that needed maintenance. Placed remotely at the time of departure, they would go to great lengths and expenses to be transferred to the domes where their skill set was valued.

Guyen had a jerry-rigged tel-screen and microphone. Everything that amplified the voice or broadcast image was jerry-rigged; the Hosts had nothing in place for communication between the variations of Humans they had evolved. This helped foster cooperation between all variations after the Occupation, as the Bugs would rely on Borrowers to relay messages to Dolls and Halflings, who could relay messages to the Humans and Goliaths.

The message Guyen had for her was not unexpected. In truth, she had gleaned it from his tiny blinking presence. Still, some general sense of other minds in the room had become habitual. They could promise not to use thoughtspeak on the little humans.

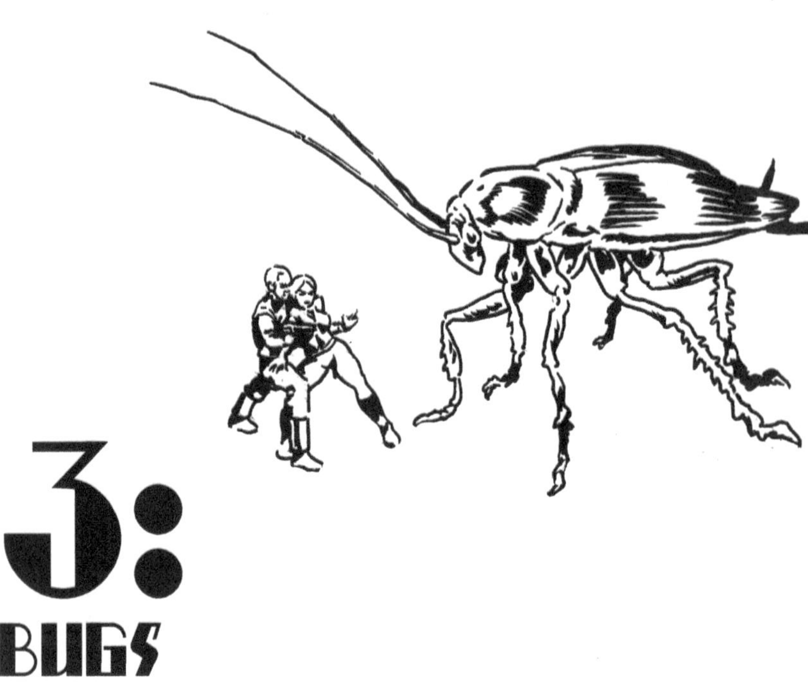

3: BUGS

Sra found Guyen in the spacious lounge area, a few inches of an empty room at the dome edge, its glass un opaqued to provide a sweeping view of the mixed variation quarter, the massive outbuildings of the Dome, the miles of farmland, and the majestic woods and mountains beyond.

The Dome mechanism sapped resources from deep within the Earth, rumored to be rooted in its core. The rest of the planet was left to heal during the Occupation. A few base-sized humans worked the farms in fewer numbers than their populations before the Occupation. The ravenous Goliaths, created to build the Domes' massive outbuildings, were an even smaller population. Of the smaller races, able to live on much fewer resources, the most populous were the Bugs, countless trillions around every Dome, with Hives placed near Host technology worldwide.

All their living and leisure spaces were enormous by their standards. They only had to endure tight squeezes at work within the Alien's endless worming cords and tubes.

Sra and Guyen were alone in the lounge as the evening light threw the spare details of the room into shadow relief. The morning shift was tubing home already, and the night shift was establishing themselves at their stations.

Sra's mind was abuzz from her day at work. A Mega baby's formula tap had needed repair. She spent the day bouncing and flying from one end of the enormous crib-nook to another, accessing the spout and the panel on either side. To her amazement, a care-droid even wheeled the baby in to watch her. The Mega baby, a massive Bhuda demi-god, briefly cooed and laughed at the little figure flittering back and forth in his nook.

Guyen also emanated vibes of barely contained energy gone systematic. They both were sipping fizz from the tap, creating a smooth, slippery smaze over their work buzz. Lightly gripping the bar or hooking a toe under the ridge beneath, they drifted up and pulled themselves down.

"See anything interesting on the job today?" Guyen grinned at her. "Why yes," and she described the gigantic infant and his acres of crib.

"How about you? Anything interesting today in the gravity engines?"

"As a matter of fact," he passed her the chip. "This is all backed up at my station here. Why don't you take that home and have a look, see if you come to the same conclusions I did."

"I don't usually work the Gravity engines."

"It's the same basic principle as the food replicators and the rest of the Dome tech, just a bit more elaborate. Give it a look; I think you'll figure it out," he smiled.

She smiled back and took the chip, buttoning it into her coverall. Seeking his eyes, she unbuttoned from a more northern location on the coverall.

"Have you ever had sex in low gravity?" she asked while unhooking her toe from the rim and floating away from the bar. "I've heard there are some positions that would be... Otherwise impossible." A smile lit his face, and Guyen disengaged from the bar and floated toward her.

"Let's find out."

4: THE FUTURE

Deaze reported back to her supervisors via thoughtspeak.

Does anyone else know?

Only the Bug engineer and myself.

The order came back more abstract than verbal. An image of a human swatting a mosquito or roughly pinching a flea off their skin.

Deaze reached out, sort of humming subvocalized thoughtspeak to herself. She gradually expanded the depth of the thought-hum but not the amplitude, if you will. She became aware of the voices and thoughts of all of the lower humans in the Dome as one hears chirping birds in the trees of an arboretum. She narrowed her focus, feeling just the swarming Bugs in the Dome's walls. In a reach more akin to smelling than listening, like a snake tasting the air, she found Guyen as he entered the tube outside the Dome that would bring the man almost to his doorway. Located, she could directly send a mind spider to creep around his memory to find knowledge he'd gained that day. Once tasted and smelled, the knowledge engram could convey the sensation to others. She mentally flagged Guyen as she sniffed around the Bug population. No one else yet had acquired the knowledge. The Bug hadn't told anyone.

She had liked the little gravity engineer. And his skills are still needed to maintain the gravity engines for years.

But there would always be a trillion bugs ready to take his place. In Sra's mind's eye, the Mega formed the image of a finger poised to flick a gnat off her arm.

Guyen sat back in the tube with a satisfied grin. Sra was really something. He hoped he'd see her again soon. He looked around. The encounter had almost taken today's discovery off his mind. The implications for the future were astounding. There really was no reason not to just tell someone about it. It was fun to be coy with Sra knowing she would enjoy examining the data in the chip. But there was a simple fact he could relay to anyone, starting right now. This would, after all, change everything for everyone, especially the Bugs, but also for all the humans worldwide.

He turned to speak to his seat neighbor and then violently spasmed, his body lurching as if a giant finger had just flicked him upside the head. He slumped in his seat.

Sra arrived back in her apartment. It was one-half of the spaces the Hosts had built to house the tiny humans that encircled their domes, renovated into simply comfortable rather than cavernous. It was enough for her, though sometimes she wished she were base sized human so she could have a cat. She often watched cat videos broadcast from The Farm and found the furry creatures adorable.

She popped the chip into a view feeder and studied it while eating a bowl from the food tap.

Guyen had been right. She had little difficulty interpreting the data, and the truth was inescapable. It would take perhaps a hundred years, but the artificial gravity in the Dome would not last forever in their Host's absence. They would eventually need to join their counterparts on the Moon or Mars, or the Megas on Earth would die.

An astonished and eager smile crossed her face.

The Giants would not inherit the Earth.

MIKE DUBISCH has been creating and publishing comics and art since the 1980's. Dubisch has carved out a unique place for himself in the world of art and comics, creating works of horror, science-fiction, surrealism, and ya adventure using all but lost traditional techniques. Born in California, USA, the artist has traveled the world and lived in five countries. Dubisch has been an instructor at the Academy of Art University since 2012, and is married to children's book illustrator and sculptor Carolyn Watson Dubisch with whom he has three daughters.

www.ingramcontent.com/pod-product-compliance
Lightning Source LLC
Chambersburg PA
CBHW030336310726
48979CB00001B/59
* 9 7 8 1 9 6 0 2 1 3 0 5 1 *